THE SUN'S ASLEEP BEHIND THE HILL

adapted from an Armenian song by
Mirra Ginsburg

illustrated by
Paul O. Zelinsky

Greenwillow Books
New York

Library of Congress
Cataloging in Publication Data

Ginsburg, Mirra.
The sun's asleep behind the hill.
Summary: The sun, the
breeze, the leaves, the
bird, the squirrel, and
the child all grow tired
after a long day and go
to sleep.
[1. Bedtime—Fiction.
2. Night—Fiction.
3. Stories in rhyme]
I. Zelinsky, Paul O., ill.
II. Title.
PZ8.3.G424Su   [E]   81-6615
ISBN 0-688-00824-0   AACR2
ISBN 0-688-00825-9 (lib. bdg.)

To Polya and Alik
—M.G.

To Deborah
—P. O. Z.

The sun shone
in the sky all day.

The sun grew tired
and went away

to sleep behind the hill.

The breeze blew
in the trees all day.
The breeze grew tired
and said:

"The sun shone
in the sky all day.
The sun grew tired
and went away
to sleep behind the hill.

"It's time that I was still."

The leaves shook
in the breeze all day.
The leaves grew tired
and said:

"The breeze blew
in the trees all day.
The breeze grew tired,
the breeze is still.

"Now we can also rest."

The bird sang
in the bush all day.
The bird grew tired
and said:

"The leaves shook
in the breeze all day.
The leaves grew tired,
they do not shake,
they are asleep
over the lake.

"Now I must also rest."

The squirrel leaped
from branch to branch.
She gathered nuts all day.
The squirrel grew very tired
and said:

"The bird sang
in the bush all day.
The bird grew tired,
the bird is quiet.

"Now I must also rest."

The child played
in the park all day.
The child grew tired.
His mother said:

"The squirrel leaped
from branch to branch.
She gathered nuts all day.
The squirrel grew very,
    very tired,
  she's sleeping in her nest.

"It's time for you to rest."

The moon came out
into the sky.

"I am alone!" she said.
"The sun's asleep
behind the hill.
The breeze is still.
The leaves don't shake,
they are asleep
over the lake.
The bird is quiet.
The squirrel is sleeping
in her nest.
The child's at rest.

"I am alone.
And I will shine
with a silver light,

in the wide, silent sky
all night."